MEGAN IN ANCIENT GREECE
by Susan Korman

Illustrations by
Bill Dodge

Spot Illustrations by
Catherine Huerta

MAGIC ATTIC PRESS

Published by Magic Attic Press.

For more information contact:
Book Editor, Magic Attic Press, 866 Spring Street,
Westbrook, ME 04092-3038

First Edition
Printed in the United States of America
1 2 3 4 5 6 7 8 9 10

Magic Attic Club® is a registered trademark.

Betsy Gould, Publisher
Marva Martin, Art Director
Jay Brady, Managing Editor

Edited by Judit Bodnar
Designed by Cindy Vacek

Korman, Susan
Megan in Ancient Greece / by Susan Korman:
illustrations by Bill Dodge, spot illustrations by Catherine Huerta
(Magic Attic Club)
Summary: Megan finds herself in ancient Greece when everyone is getting ready to
celebrate the Festival of the Harvest. She discovers that the statue of Demeter has been
stolen from the temple. Can Megan find the thieves in time to save the statue?
ISBN 1-57513-128-5 (hardback) ISBN 1-57513-127-7 (paperback)
ISBN 1-57513-143-9 (library edition hardback)

Library of Congress Cataloging in Publication Data is on file at the Library of Congress

As members of the
MAGIC ATTIC CLUB,
we promise to
be best friends,
share all of our adventures in the attic,
use our imaginations,
have lots of fun together,
and remember—the real magic is in us.

Alison   Keisha

Heather   Megan

Rose

Table of Contents

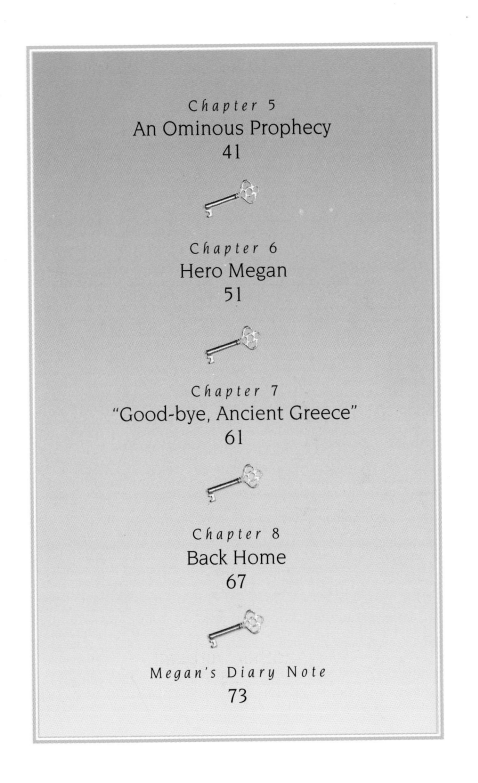

Megan in Ancient Greece
Prologue

When Alison, Heather, Keisha, and Megan find a golden key buried in the snow, they have no idea that it will change their lives forever. They discover that it belongs to Ellie Goodwin, the owner of an old Victorian house across the street from Alison's. Ellie, grateful when they return the key to her, invites the girls to play in her attic. There they find a steamer trunk filled with wonderful outfits—party dresses, a princess gown, a ballet tutu, cowgirl clothes, and many, many, more. The girls try on some of the costumes and admire their reflections in a tall, gilded mirror nearby. Suddenly they are transported to a new time and place, embarking on the greatest adventure of their lives.

After they return to the present and Ellie's attic, they form the Magic Attic Club, promising to tell each other every exciting detail of their future adventures. Then they meet Rose Hopkins, a new girl at school, and invite her to join the club and share their amazing secret.

Chapter One

THE BEST-MADE PLANS

eather?" Megan Ryder said, checking the neatly typed list in front of her on the cafeteria table. "You're bringing spider cookies to the hayride tomorrow, right?"

"That's right," Heather Hardin told her friend cheerfully. She smoothed her long, brown hair and adjusted the scrunchie, which matched her blue sweater. "It took my mom and me forever to bake enough for everyone. But that's because my dad was eating them as fast as we made them," she added with a grin.

Megan was already checking the next item on her list. "Keisha, are the decorations for the hay wagon ready?"

"Yes," Keisha Vance reported. "They're all finished, and my father even offered to drive Kristen and me to the farm first thing tomorrow morning. Don't worry," she added reassuringly, "we'll have the wagon ready way before everyone else arrives."

Megan breathed a sigh of relief. Getting the decorations ready was one less thing she had to worry about now.

"The wagon is going to look amazing, Megan," Kristen Gannon told her. "Keisha and I made bats out of black posterboard, and we used glow-in-the-dark paint for the fake tombstones."

"Cool!" Alison McCann exclaimed. Her blue eyes blazed with excitement from under the brim of her baseball cap. "That stuff sounds pretty spooky."

"It is," Keisha said. "I..."

Megan didn't hear the rest of the conversation; she was too busy checking off the next few things on her long list of things to do. It was after school on Friday and a group of fifth-graders was meeting in the cafeteria with Mrs. North, the class adviser. The entire grade was going on a haunted hayride at Appleby's Farm the next day, and

Megan was in charge of planning the event. She was a very organized person, and good at details, but this was a big job. She kept worrying that she'd lose track of who was making refreshments, or doing the clean-up, or calling all the parents. Luckily, her four best friends in the Magic Attic Club—Heather, Keisha, Alison, and Rose— were being a big help.

"I can't wait until tomorrow," Rose Hopkins was saying. "Everyone is going to be so spooked when Mr. Appleby drives the wagon past that dancing skeleton."

"And when his son gallops across the field disguised as the headless horseman," Alison piped up. "Even Joey Diaz is going to be scared."

A few kids grinned. Joey was always bragging about how brave he was.

"I bet Joey will be so scared, he'll lose *his* head," Rose joked.

Laughter erupted at the table. Soon everybody was cracking headless horseman jokes.

Finally, Megan held up a hand. "Come on, guys," she reminded the others. "We still have work to do."

After the meeting Megan walked home with her friends. On the way they talked about tryouts for the basketball team, which were being held the following week.

"I hope I make the team," Rose said. She was wearing jeans and a bright blue football jacket, which set off her dark brown eyes. "We didn't have one at my old school."

"You'll make the team," Keisha reassured her. "Just about everyone who tries out makes it."

"Which is a good thing," Heather chimed in with a laugh, "because I'm not very good at dribbling or shooting baskets!"

Megan was glad that Rose was trying out for the team, too. Basketball would be a lot more fun if she was playing. She had just enrolled in their school, but already had become close friends with Megan and the others, and was the newest member of the Magic Attic Club.

"The basketball team is lots of fun," Alison was saying. "The coach is really nice, and we'll have a game every Wednesday at the gym…"

Megan tried to follow the conversation, but her mind was full of everything she still had to do to get ready for the hayride. She had to remind Mr. Appleby this morning to tell him how many kids were coming. She had to remind Jack Stevens to bring apple cider, and tell Joey Diaz not to forget to wear his vampire costume.

"Don't you think so, Megan?"

"Huh?" Megan startled as she realized that someone had just said something to her. "What did you say?" she asked, looking at her friends.

"Earth to Megan!" Heather teased her.

"You were in outer space!" Alison declared.

Rose looked at her friend closely. "Are you okay? You seem so distracted."

"I *am* distracted," Megan confessed with a sigh. "I've got so much to do by tomorrow. I don't want to forget anything."

Keisha draped an arm around Megan's shoulder. "The hayride's going to be great, Megan. Stop worrying about it."

Rose nodded. "You heard Mrs. North. You're doing a great job."

"Can you imagine if I were the one in charge?" Alison said, rolling her eyes. "I'd lose my lists, forget to tell kids to bring the refreshments…oh, gosh," she went on, "I'd probably even forget the hay!"

"Hay?" Keisha echoed in confusion.

"You know, for the *hayride*," Alison said.

Keisha giggled and nudged Alison gently with her elbow. Alison pretended to go flying forward on the sidewalk.

Megan laughed. She knew that her friends were acting goofy on purpose. They were trying to make her laugh, to help her stop being such a worrywart.

"You guys are the best," she told them. "Thanks."

"You're welcome," Heather told her warmly.

The girls turned down Primrose Lane. By the time they stopped in front of Megan's tall white colonial house, she had managed to convince herself that Mrs. North was right, and so were her friends. Thanks to her hard work, the fifth-grade hayride was going to be the best event of the school year!

Chapter
Two

RAIN, RAIN, GO AWAY!

egan?" a voice called softly the next morning. "Are you awake, honey?"

Megan rolled over in bed and slowly opened one eye. Her mother stood in the doorway wearing her Saturday uniform—an old pair of gray sweats and a baggy white sweatshirt. Her hair was pulled back from her face.

"Morning, Mom," Megan mumbled sleepily. She sat up and glanced at the digital clock radio on her nightstand. It said seven-thirteen. "I'm glad you woke me up early. I've got so much to do today."

"Actually, honey…"

Megan opened both eyes. This time, as she looked at her mother, she noticed an odd expression on her face.

"I'm not sure about…" her mother hesitated. "The hayride…" Looking uneasy, Megan's mother finally just pointed to the window.

Megan pushed aside the yellow stenciled coverlet on her bed and dashed over to the window. Peering outside, she saw for herself: The sky was foggy and gray. A heavy rain fell in torrents, slashing at the windowpane.

"Oh no!" Megan's stomach suddenly felt hollow. She looked at her mother in a panic. "It's pouring!"

"Why don't we go downstairs and listen to the weather report?" Megan's mother suggested. "The hayride doesn't start until four-thirty. Maybe the rain will stop by then."

Megan threw on her bathrobe and slippers, then raced down to the kitchen. Her Aunt Frances was reading the paper and sipping coffee at the table.

"Have you heard a weather report yet, Aunt Frances?" Megan burst out.

Her aunt looked up from her paper. The radio on the counter was already tuned to a news station.

"It's going to be a gloomy weekend in our area, folks," the weather lady announced suddenly. "Expect heavy rain

and winds today through Monday afternoon. It's a perfect
weekend to get some housecleaning done, or go to a movie."

Megan slumped into a chair. For a moment, she
didn't know whether to laugh or burst into sobs. All this
time she'd been worried that *she* would make a mistake,
or forget to do something on her list. It had never once
occurred to her that weather would ruin everyone's plans.

She could feel her mother and aunt looking at her.

"Why don't you call the owner of the farm and see if you
can reschedule?" Aunt Frances suggested, pulling her green
velour bathrobe a little tighter. "Maybe you can postpone
the hayride till next weekend, or the following one."

Megan rested her chin on one of her hands, deep in
thought. Some of the snacks would have to be made all
over again, but the decorations could be saved. There really
isn't any reason why we can't reschedule, she decided.

"That's a good idea, Aunt Frances," Megan responded,
glancing at the clock. It's only seven-thirty, but farmers
are supposed to rise early, she thought. Mr. Appleby must
be awake by now.

Megan found his phone number on one of her lists,
and dialed.

Mr. Appleby didn't seem at all surprised to hear from
her. "Too bad about the weather," he said sympathetically.

Megan told him about her idea to reschedule. "Can
we have the hayride next weekend instead?" she asked.

17

"Oh, I don't know about that," the farmer replied. "Fall is my busy season. I'm pretty sure we're booked every weekend from now until Thanksgiving."

"Oh." Megan felt her spirits sink.

"But hold on for a minute while I check the calendar," Mr. Appleby added. "My wife usually handles our schedule, and I could be wrong."

Megan held her breath, praying that Mr. Appleby would return to the phone with good news. But as soon as he began to speak again, Megan knew that wasn't the case at all.

"I'm sorry, Megan. As I suspected, we can't fit you in for another haunted hayride this fall."

"Are you sure?" Megan said pleadingly. "Everyone's going to be so disappointed."

"Yes, honey, I'm sure they are," the farmer replied. "But I do have another idea. If you and your classmates want to come up here next Wednesday after school, we can take you over to the pumpkin patch to pick pumpkins. And I bet we can arrange for a ride around the farm on our antique fire truck, too. It's got a really loud bell," he added with a chuckle.

A *fire truck*? A *trip to the pumpkin patch*? Megan couldn't believe what Mr. Appleby was suggesting. She knew he was trying to be nice, but he was acting as if they were kindergarteners.

Still, she did her best to be
polite. "I'll talk to the teachers
about your idea and call you
back on Monday," she managed
to say.

Megan's next phone call
was to Mrs. North. The teacher
was more enthusiastic about Mr.
Appleby's suggestion. "It's certainly
different," she pointed out. "And you
know something? Everyone might think it's fun."

"Fun?" Megan repeated. "Excuse me, Mrs. North, but I
don't think so. I haven't been interested in fire trucks
since I was three years old!"

To Megan's surprise, Mrs. North laughed. "I know it's
not exactly what you had in mind," she said calmly. "But
it sounds as if we don't have much choice. Unless you
want to cancel the event altogether."

"No." Megan sighed. "I guess not."

"Why don't we all meet on Monday and talk it over?
Maybe someone will have another idea. In the meantime,
we'll have to let everyone know that thanks to Mother
Nature, the hayride is cancelled," the teacher said.

Megan spent the next hour or so making phone calls
to spread the word. Several kids asked if the ride was
going to be rescheduled. Megan didn't have the heart to

tell them the truth—that it looked as if they'd be riding around the farm on a fire truck clanging a bell like three-year-olds instead of taking a spooky ride through the dark woods. Each time someone asked her about it, she mumbled something about talking it over on Monday, then got off the phone as quickly as she could.

After lunch, Megan headed back upstairs to her room. She flipped on the radio, then stretched out on her bed next to her cat, Ginger. The cat purred contentedly as Megan stroked her soft calico fur.

"Why did it have to rain today, Ginger?" Megan sighed. "After all my hard work."

Just then a knock sounded on the door.

"Come in," Megan called.

"Hey, Megs." Aunt Frances poked her head into the room. "Want to check out the new bookstore in town with me? I heard it has a café that serves caramel hot chocolate—with real whipped cream!" she added temptingly.

Megan shook her head. "No, thanks, Aunt Frances."

"No, thanks?" Aunt Frances clasped a hand over her heart dramatically, and pretended to swoon.

In spite of her gloomy mood, Megan grinned. Aunt Frances had moved in with Megan and her mother a few years earlier, shortly after Megan's parents

were divorced, and Megan loved having her around. Aunt Frances liked adventurous outdoor sports and trying new things. Her latest project was a workshop for amateur actors at the Community Center. Ever since she'd joined the group, she'd been talking in foreign accents and funny voices, and pretending to be characters from famous movies.

"Mercy me," her aunt drawled, imitating a southern belle. "Can it be true that Megan Ryder, the world's biggest reader, is turning down the chance to visit a bookstore?" She draped a hand over Megan's forehead. "You must be delirious with fever!"

Megan sat up and giggled. "Thanks," she said. "It was a really nice offer, but I think I'll take you up on it another time. Today I just feel like lying around and feeling sorry for myself."

"Are you sure, honey?" Aunt Frances asked, acting like herself again. "I'm very good company, you know."

"I do know that," Megan told her. "But I'm sure."

"Okay, then," her aunt said. "But if you change your mind, I'll be downstairs. You know, Megs," she added softly, "you can't do anything about the rain, and it might do you some good to get out." With that, she gave a little wave and shut the bedroom door.

Megan moped around a bit longer. But by two-thirty, she still felt irritable—and bored to tears. "You know what?" she said to Ginger. "Aunt Frances is right. I should go out for a little while."

But she still wasn't in the mood to go to the bookstore. As she rummaged around in her closet, looking for her umbrella, she had another destination in mind: Ellie Goodwin's house.

C h a p t e r

Three

THE GREEK MAIDEN

ello, Megan," Ellie said, opening the front door of her white Victorian house. "It's still raining cats and dogs out there, isn't it?"

"It sure is." Megan shook out her soaked umbrella, then stepped into the foyer, glad to be out of the cold fall rain. Ellie was dressed in a heavy wool sweater she'd brought back from a recent trip to Ireland and a pair of fuzzy pink slippers. Megan dropped her umbrella in the stand near the door, and followed her friend into the kitchen. She told Ellie all about the cancelled hayride.

"That's too bad," Ellie said sympathetically. "If it's any comfort, the weather ruined my plans for today, too. A friend and I were supposed to go hiking in the woods."

Megan sank into a rose-colored chair at the table. Ellie had painted each one in a different color of a Western sunset. "Were you disappointed you couldn't go?" Megan asked.

"Oh, yes," Ellie said. "But I couldn't do anything about the rain, so I made the best of things." She pointed to the stove, where a large pot was simmering. "I made soup with the zucchini and tomatoes from my garden."

For the first time, Megan was aware of the delicious aroma wafting through the air.

"Well, I spent most of the day being angry with Mother Nature," Megan confessed. "That's why I came over to your house. Do you think it'd be all right if I went upstairs for a while?"

"Of course." Ellie stirred the vegetable soup and smiled. "I have a feeling that a trip to the attic will put everything in a different light."

A few moments later, Megan retrieved the golden key from the box in the foyer and unlocked the door leading to the attic. As she stepped into the room, she felt a tingle of excitement all over. Whenever she or any of her friends in the Magic Attic Club opened the old steamer trunk in the attic, they found all kinds of wonderful outfits inside—ballgowns, silky harem pants, gymnast leotards. They never knew what adventures were in store, and Megan couldn't wait to see what she'd discover today.

Megan reached for the satin cord on the overhead lamp and flipped on the light. She hurried across the room and knelt beside the open trunk. There was no way she could miss the brightly colored feather attached to a long wand that rested on top.

Megan picked up the feathered object. "It's a fan," she murmured. Her eyes flicked back to the white garment inside the trunk. That looked interesting, too. It had a gold corded belt and its sleeves and hem were trimmed in gold.

She reached into the trunk and pulled out the dress. As she shook it out, she realized it was a tunic, or *chiton*, just like the ones worn by the people of ancient Greece. In school, Megan had loved learning about the Classical Age, a time more than two thousand years earlier when art, architecture, literature, and drama had flourished in

Greek civilization. She had especially enjoyed studying the Greek myths, wonderful stories about mighty gods who ruled the earth from Mount Olympus.

Eagerly, Megan kicked off her sneakers and jeans, slipped on the *chiton* and tied the belt. She put on the matching cape made of sheer, white fabric with gold trim and golden sandals that she found in the trunk, then hurried over to the tall, gilt-edged mirror. Still holding the feathered fan, she studied her reflection. Gazing back at her was a young girl...

Who looks just like a Greek maiden! Megan thought with a smile.

All at once the walls of Ellie's attic faded. Megan found herself outdoors under a hot morning sun.

"Fish! Fresh fish from the sea!" "Fruit!" "Bread!" voices shouted.

Megan looked around cautiously. She had arrived at a busy marketplace that was bursting with noise. All around her, vendors stood near wooden stalls selling bread, olives, beans, fruit, and other foods. Each man loudly shouted the price of his goods, trying to outdo the others. A group of fishermen displayed the morning's catch in large baskets overflowing with fish. Chickens squawked noisily, and the squeals of pigs filled the air. Dozens of craftsmen were peddling their wares— handwoven baskets, ceramic jugs for wine and water,

small statues, and cooking pots.

With a start, Megan realized that she'd seen illustrations of this place in her textbook at school. She'd arrived at the famous *agora*, or marketplace, in Athens, Greece. She could hardly believe it, but she'd traveled over two thousand years into the past!

Just then two men walked past, leading a donkey. Megan jumped back to get out of their way.

"There is the new temple," she heard one say.

The men stopped.

Megan's eyes followed the man's finger as he pointed to a hill in the distance. A beautiful building made of white marble rose majestically above the crest of the hill. Its tall columns were decorated with gold paint, which glinted in the sunlight.

"So that is Nestor's fine Temple of Demeter, the building that is the talk of Athens," said the other man.

Surprised by his harsh tone, Megan glanced over. He was younger than his companion, with dark hair and an athletic build. A long purple scar ran down his left cheek. "Well, soon the citizens of Athens won't be talking about the temple's beauty," the man went on. "Tonight, after darkness falls, we will return and make sure that—"

"Baskets! Fine straw baskets!"

A vendor with a cartload of woven items stopped in front of Megan. His loud cries drowned out the rest of the man's words.

As the vendor moved on, Megan caught a last bit of the men's conversation.

"I am weary from our journey from Sparta. Let's rest before we discuss our plans," the younger man said.

Megan watched as the two men continued on their way with their donkey. As they disappeared into the crowd, an uneasy feeling settled over her. Why had the younger man seemed so upset by the temple? she wondered. Was she imagining things, or had...

A sharp voice startled her out of her thoughts.

"Mistress Megala!"

Megan looked up to see a tall, thin girl hurrying toward her. She was barefoot and wore a plain white *chiton* with no jewelry. On her arm was a large basket heaped with fish, grapes, apples, and pears.

The girl looked worried. "We'd better go, mistress," the girl urged her. "We have lingered much too long. Your Aunt Cassia will be very angry if we are not home soon with the provisions for tonight's banquet. Come," she added, hurrying away from the busy square.

Obediently, Megan followed. As they walked along, Megan tried to learn more about where they were going and what would happen there. "Did you say that the banquet is tonight?" she asked.

The girl stopped and looked at her quizzically. "Your

Aunt Cassia is right," she declared. "You do spend too much time with your head in the clouds like the philosophers." The girl laughed. "Of course the banquet is tonight, mistress. It will be a wonderful celebration," she went on excitedly. "Your Uncle Lysius and Cousin Nestor have built such a beautiful temple for Demeter. Everyone is saying that they are the finest architects in all of Athens."

"Oh—right," Megan mumbled. Her question had almost given away the fact that she didn't really belong there. She waved the fan, pretending to cool herself. "I think I am tired from the hot sun," she said, hoping that would explain her behavior.

The other girl shrugged. To Megan's relief she didn't say anything more.

As the girls resumed walking, Megan remembered that the two men at the *agora* had been talking about the Temple of Demeter, too. Demeter was a very important goddess to the ancient Greeks. She was the goddess of the harvest, the kind and generous Mother Earth who was responsible for the changing seasons and bountiful crops.

Pointing to the basket on her companion's arm, Megan asked, "Is that what we will eat at the banquet? I hope so," she added politely. "Fish is one of my favorite—"

The girl burst out laughing. "Things must be very different in your city-state, mistress. Your uncle has certainly not invited me or any of his other slaves to dine with him. And you're not invited, either," she added, shooting a sly look at Megan. "As always, the feast is only for the men."

Megan cringed, her face red with embarrassment. Now that she looked more closely, she realized that the girl's *chiton* was threadbare and smudged with dirt in several spots. She was a servant, of course—but it hadn't even occurred to Megan that she might be a slave.

"Right," Megan mumbled. "I…" Her words trailed off helplessly. She'd been in ancient Greece for less than an hour, and already she'd said two very dumb things. From now on, she'd have to be more careful about what she said, or someone was going to guess her secret!

Chapter
Four

ANOTHER OUTBURST

egan looked around curiously as she followed her companion through Athens. Plain, solid-looking homes made of mud brick lined the streets. Here and there were more elaborate buildings with tall columns painted in vibrant scarlet, green, and gold. Sculpted busts adorned several of the street corners.

At last the servant girl stopped in front of a one-story house. Megan was about to step into it when the girl touched her arm. "Wait, Mistress Megala," she warned her. "Here in Athens, we cross the threshold with the right foot first. This brings good luck to the household."

Megan did as the girl said. Then she followed her along a narrow passageway, which opened up into a central outdoor court.

"There you are, Alexia," a tall, attractive woman with braided hair declared. She must be Aunt Cassia, Megan thought. "You were gone for a very long time," the older woman chided. She frowned at Megan. "Megala, you know that it is not proper for a girl of your age to be out in public for so long. I expected you home quite some time ago."

Megan hesitated, trying to think of a way to apologize for being late. To her relief, Alexia came to her rescue.

"The marketplace was very crowded today, Mistress Cassia," Alexia said quickly. "Many visitors are in Athens for the Festival of the Eleusinian Mysteries. That is why it took so long for us to fetch the food for the banquet. Look at this, mistress," she added before Cassia could say anything more.

Aunt Cassia's frown turned to a delighted smile when she saw the basket of food in Alexia's arms.

"Megala and I have brought back some excellent fish for tonight's banquet. The men can feast on mackerel and sturgeon—and I paid very little for it," Alexia added proudly.

Cassia beamed at her. "Splendid, Alexia. That is why I

like to send you to the marketplace instead of my husband. You are always able to get such good prices from the fish vendors."

Cassia took the basket from the slave girl and started for the kitchen. "Come along, Alexia," she said. "We must begin the preparations for tonight's feast."

"May I help with anything?" Megan asked.

"Thank you for your kind offer, Megala," Aunt Cassia replied. "I do not need help in the kitchen, but I'm sure that your cousin Penelope"—she gestured to a girl who sat a short distance away—"would be glad of some help with her weaving."

The teenage girl looked up and waved Megan over. Dressed in a deep purple *chiton*, Penelope had dark hair and brown eyes, like her mother.

"Mother's right, Megala," Penelope said, smiling. "I would be glad to take a short rest." She stood up and handed over a spindle and another tool that Megan had never seen before.

Megan panicked as she sat on the ground beside her cousin. What am I going to do? I've watched people using spinning wheels, she thought, remembering her adventure as a medieval princess with a unicorn, but that's no help to me. This is completely different!

For a moment, she just sat there, holding the unfamiliar tools.

"Are you all right?" Penelope asked her.

"I'm fine," Megan answered quickly. As she looked down at the tools in her hand, her fingers suddenly knew what to do. Deftly she dangled the long strand of wool and let it spin into a fine thread. Relief washed over her as her hands did the work. She shouldn't have worried, she reminded herself. Often when she was on an adventure, she found herself with a new talent.

Penelope rested for a few minutes. Then she began combing wool, talking about the lovely colors she would use to dye it later on. As they worked, Megan asked

Penelope about the Festival of the Eleusinian Mysteries.

"As you know, Cousin, it is to honor the goddess of the harvest. We offer gifts and hope that she will reward us with food, as well as warmth and light when springtime comes. It only takes place every five years," Penelope added."It is fortunate that you are in Athens to see such an important event." She smiled warmly at Megan.

"I'm really looking forward to going to the celebration with you," Megan replied.

"The dedication of the temple will be held tomorrow, on the first day of the festival," Penelope went on eagerly. "I am so glad that Father has allowed us to attend. Now that I am fifteen, I am rarely permitted outside our home, and I have never even seen my father and brother's temple."

"I'm sure it will be very exciting." Megan kept her eyes on her work, careful not to reveal her surprise that Penelope stayed indoors all the time. "Will there be many special ceremonies during the festival?" she asked.

"Oh yes," Penelope replied. "After the temple dedication, the crowd will proceed together to the sacred site of Eleusis. There we will perform the sacred mysteries to honor Demeter."

Megan knew that if she asked what "mysteries" Penelope was talking about, it would make her cousin suspicious. So she kept the rest of her questions to herself, and continued with the weaving and wool-dyeing for the rest of the morning. When a servant announced that it was lunchtime, Megan felt her stomach rumble. She was starving!

Aunt Cassia was waiting for the girls in the dining chamber, where they ate a simple meal of grapes, apples, bread, and olives. As the women were finishing their lunch, two men entered the room.

Penelope smiled at them, "Hello, Father. Hello, Nestor."

"Good evening, my wife and daughter," the older man said. He was tall and partially bald, with a graying beard. "And to you, too, niece," he added, smiling at Megan. "I hope your day in Athens has been pleasant so far."

"Very pleasant, Uncle Lysius," Megan replied politely.

Nestor was tall and handsome, and he flashed Megan a friendly grin. "I hope that my cousin is getting ready for the dedication of the Temple of Demeter tomorrow."

"Oh, I am," Megan blurted out. Without thinking, she added, "But I wish we were invited to tonight's banquet, too. It sounds so—"

"Megala!" Aunt Cassia gasped. Penelope stared at her

in disbelief. A shocked silence filled the room.

"That's enough of such talk, Megala," Uncle Lysius said kindly but firmly. "The women will stay out of sight while the guests are here. That is the way things are done."

Megan looked down, feeling her face turn as red as the skin of the apple on her plate. Once again she'd managed to put her foot in her mouth.

But it *is* unfair that we can't go to the banquet, she thought stubbornly.

Looking up, she noticed Nestor watching her. As their eyes met, he gave her an amused smile.

Megan smiled back, glad that at least one person in the room wasn't horrified by her outburst.

After lunch, Megan and Penelope helped Aunt Cassia tidy the house. When they were finished, the two girls went back to weaving. As they worked, Megan felt restless and a little bored. It was hard to sit still, knowing that outside the walls of the house, the rest of Athens was bustling with preparations for the festival. She wished she could find a way to get out for a while.

It was late in the afternoon when Megan got her chance. Handing her an urn, Aunt Cassia asked her to help Alexia fetch water from the public fountain.

"Of course, Aunt Cassia," Megan

replied eagerly. She quickly set down her weaving tools and hurried after the servant. As they joined the crowd streaming toward the marketplace, Megan felt her spirits rise. It was certainly a lot more fun to be outside, where all the excitement was.

Chapter

Five

AN OMINOUS PROPHECY

oon Megan passed a large, open-air theater crowded with spectators.

"What's going on?" Megan asked Alexia. As she peered around the stone bleachers, she noticed several men strutting about on a stage. Their faces were covered by masks.

"The actors are performing a

drama in honor of the goddess Demeter," Alexia explained.

"Can we watch?" Megan asked eagerly.

Alexia shook her head. "We cannot linger outside today, mistress. Your aunt will be very angry if we return home late again."

Megan knew that Alexia was right. Still, she wished they could stay and watch the performance.

By the time the girls reached the *agora*, Megan was very hot. Alexia led her to a *stoa*, one of the covered walkways that surrounded the open square. "Let's rest here in the shade for a moment before we continue on to the fountain," she suggested.

Megan nodded, glad for the chance to be out of the sun. As they rested, she looked around the *stoa* in awe. Now I know why it's called the "painted porch," she thought. Almost the entire length of the inner wall was covered with vivid artwork depicting a glorious battle.

Megan quickly realized that she and Alexia weren't the only ones who'd sought out the porch to get out of the sun. It was crowded with small groups of men and boys, talking and arguing. A crier walked up and down its length, announcing that someone had lost a valuable bracelet. Another crier called out the price of an animal for sale. Megan spotted a barber shop and what looked like a physician's waiting room. The scene was so crowded and lively, she could barely take in everything happening around her.

Suddenly she noticed a young man with dark hair walking toward her.

"Nestor!" she called, smiling and waving to get his attention. She was excited to see her cousin.

But Nestor just stared straight ahead, as if he hadn't heard her. As he drew closer, Megan saw that he looked troubled.

She hurried toward him. "Nestor, what's wrong?"

"Oh, Megala," he said with a start. "I was so lost in my thoughts; I did not see you. What are you doing here?" he asked.

"Aunt Cassia sent Alexia and me to fetch water from the fountain," she explained. "What's wrong?" she repeated. "You seem so upset."

"I am." Nestor sighed. "I have received very disturbing news about the temple."

"What is it?" Megan prodded. "Has something happened?"

"Not yet, but..." Nestor hesitated, as if he were trying to make up his mind about how much to say. "Alexia, please go on ahead and fetch the water. When you return, Megala can help you carry it home."

Alexia nodded, then hurried away with the urns. Megan waited for Nestor to explain what was bothering him.

He led her over to a bench. "This morning I met the farmer Prodicus," he began. "He told me that he recently visited the oracle site—and the oracle predicted that someone is going to do something to dishonor the temple. And if this person is not stopped, the goddess will be very displeased with me and Father—and with the whole city-state of Athens!"

Megan looked at him in alarm. She thought hard, trying to remember what an oracle was. Then she remembered that the ancient Greeks believed that the oracles were people who received messages from the gods, and that the gods were not only powerful but hot-tempered. No wonder Nestor looked so upset, Megan thought. He was afraid that if somebody ruined Demeter's temple, she would get angry and punish the Athenians with severe weather or a scarce harvest.

"Maybe the oracle is mistaken," Megan said hopefully.

"My father and others say that the oracles' words are pure foolishness," Nestor replied. "But as you must know, Megala, several of their prophecies *have* come true. I am fearful that Prodicus is right about this one, and that our temple is doomed."

He paced nervously. "The festival begins tomorrow," he went on. "I cannot think of anyone who bears me ill will, or would do such a thing."

Suddenly Megan remembered the two men she heard

talking about the Temple of Demeter earlier in the day. Did they have something to do with the oracle's prediction?

"Nestor," Megan began, " at the *agora*—"

But Nestor was too agitated to listen. "I don't know what to do," he interrupted. "But after eleven years of hard work, I cannot sit by and let anything spoil our magnificent building."

Megan tried again. "I saw two men yesterday and they—"

"I must go, Megala," Nestor cut her off again. "I need to find Father and talk with him again before it's too late. I will see you later, at home."

"Nestor!" Megan jumped up from the bench and called after him. But he had already disappeared into the mob of people strolling along the *stoa*.

Megan felt a prickle of worry. Maybe she was making too much of what she'd overheard, but she didn't think so. Something about those two men had given her a very uneasy feeling.

Megan hoped to see Nestor again at dinnertime, but neither he nor Uncle Lysius came home to eat. Shortly after sundown, Megan reluctantly followed Aunt Cassia and Penelope to the *gymnaikon*, the women's quarters.

Penelope climbed into bed and fell asleep right away, but Megan wasn't the least bit tired. She tossed and turned in the hard bed for what felt like hours.

I've got to do something, she thought with frustration. But what? The only time she was allowed out was when Aunt Cassia sent her on an errand.

Megan closed her eyes, listening to Penelope breathing softly. She tried to force herself to fall asleep, but worried thoughts reeled through her brain: It had taken the men eleven years to build the temple; it would be awful if something happened to it. She was sure many of the people of Athens would be horrified, too.

Megan rolled over in the hard bed, staring at the blank wall.

Suddenly, an idea came to her. She knew it was crazy, but she had to check on the temple herself. She sat up and looked around the room for something she could wear to hide the fact that she was a girl. She spotted a heavy blanket that would do the trick, draped it over her head and shoulders, and crept out of the room.

Outside, the city's narrow lanes were dark and full of shadows. The streets seemed deserted, but still Megan worried that someone would spot her.

Picking up her pace, she hurried toward the marketplace. Overhead, the moon and stars gave off enough light for her to see the hill on which the temple stood.

Megan started up the slope. As she neared the crest, she gasped. There the moon hung low, and torches burned brightly inside, bathing the marble building in an eerie white glow.

It's almost as if Demeter is guarding the temple herself, Megan thought in amazement. She stepped closer, admiring the tall, graceful columns that stood in front and along the sides of the building. Terra-cotta tiles lined the roof, each one sculpted in wheat and fruit designs. As Megan climbed the steps, she saw painted vases and bowls resting on pedestals near a stone altar. Carved into the wall behind the altar was an elaborate scene depicting the mighty gods in their golden thrones on Mount Olympus.

Omigosh, Megan thought, gazing up at the gods' chiseled faces. In the flickering torchlight, she could make out Zeus, the mighty king of the gods; Poseidon, the lord of the seas; and beautiful Aphrodite, the goddess of love. As Megan stood inside the temple beneath them, she felt as if she herself were only two inches tall.

Then she remembered why she'd come. She quickly looked around for anything suspicious. To her relief, she was alone and the temple looked fine. Maybe Nestor's friend was wrong after all, she thought.

But then something odd caught her eye. Directly in front of the altar stood a tall, scrolled pedestal. Unlike the other pedestals, which displayed bowls and statues, this one displayed nothing.

That's strange, Megan thought, stepping nearer. But before she could take a closer look, she heard a sound.

Footsteps! Her heart hammered inside her chest. Frantically, she looked around for a place to hide.

It was too late. As she tried to duck behind one of the tall columns, a shadowy figure reached the top of the steps.

"Halt!" a voice called harshly.

Megan froze in terror.

C h a p t e r
Six

HERO MEGAN

alt, intruder!" the man called.

Megan didn't move a muscle as he approached. Then, before she could react, he grabbed her roughly and tried to wrestle her to the floor. As she struggled to keep her balance, the blanket covering her head fell away.

"Megala!" the man gasped. He was so surprised that he let go of her.

"Nestor!" Megan exclaimed. "What are you doing here?"

"What are *you* doing here?" he demanded. "Surely my

mother and father do not know that you are out alone at night!"

They looked at one another, each one waiting for the other to speak first.

"I was too worried about the temple to sleep," Megan finally said.

Nestor nodded. "I was concerned as well," he confessed. His face looked pale, and his eyes were rimmed with dark shadows. "All I could think about was the prophecy."

Megan hoped it hadn't already come true. She pointed to the bare pedestal. "Has something been taken?"

Nestor gasped. "Oh, no—someone has stolen the statue of Demeter! This is just as the oracle predicted!"

"You must listen," Megan said urgently. "Yesterday at the *agora* I heard two men talking about the temple. I think they may be the thieves."

"What?" Nestor looked at her in astonishment. "Why didn't you tell me this earlier, cousin?"

"I tried," Megan explained. "But this afternoon you were in too much of a hurry to listen."

Quickly, she told him about the men's conversation.

Nestor clutched her arm. "This is important, Megala. Can you tell me what the men looked like?"

Megan thought for a moment. She remembered that both had been wearing white *chitons*, and one had mentioned being weary from their journey. "They are not from Athens," she said. "The younger man looked very strong. And he had a long scar on one cheek." She traced a line on her own cheek to show him.

"A scar?" Nestor repeated. Recognition flashed in his eyes. "It must be Antiphon!"

"Who is that?" Megan asked.

"My rival in the chariot races at the last Olympic festival," Nestor explained. "He is from the city-state of Sparta, and he expected to win. But during the race his chariot overturned and he was injured. When I was crowned champion, Antiphon was very angry."

"Do you think he's trying to get revenge?" Megan asked.

"Possibly," Nestor said, frowning. "But I have also heard talk that the Spartans are envious of our new temple to the goddess. Perhaps Antiphon is worried that now Demeter will favor Athens over Sparta."

Megan nodded, more sure than ever that this man Antiphon was the thief.

"I must stop him," Nestor said. "I was here only a short time ago, and the statue was still here. It is made of bronze," he went on. "Antiphon could not have gotten very far with such a heavy object."

"Let's go look for him," Megan urged. "I'm sure we can find him and his friend."

But Nestor shook his head. "Looking for thieves is

men's business, Megala. I know that you do not like having to stay with the women, but I fear that you have already taken too many risks. I am going to look around to make sure that nothing else has been disturbed," he added. "You must go home at once."

"But, I'm the one who told you about Antiphon and his friend," Megan protested. "You can't send me away— what if you need my help?"

"It is time for you to go home." His tone was sharp, and Megan knew better than to argue.

"Fine," she said, folding her arms stubbornly. "I will go home. But I'm sure I could help, if you'd just let me."

Nestor ignored her remark. "Here. Take this." He reached up and took down a torch. "It will light the way."

Reluctantly, Megan took the torch and said good night. As she followed one of the paths down the slope, her annoyance grew. She was getting tired of hearing that she couldn't do something just because she was a girl.

"I don't know why…" she mumbled, kicking a pebble in anger.

Megan was so lost in her thoughts, she didn't notice the large rock in the middle of her path. As her sandal struck it, she pitched forward onto the dirt.

Somehow she managed to keep the burning torch upright.

"Nice going, Megan," she said aloud.

She sat up and dusted off the palm of her free hand. As she started to get to her feet, she noticed faint marks in the dry dirt. Curious, she lowered the torch to get a closer look.

Wheel marks! she said to herself, her heart skipping a beat. As she followed the tracks a few feet, she realized that they looked fresh, as if someone had just been there.

Someone with a cart, she thought. In front of each set of marks were hoofprints. Probably left by a donkey!

Megan gazed up at the temple, unsure of what to do. Part of her knew that she should show Nestor what she'd found, but...

This is my chance, she decided.

Using her torch to see, Megan followed the tracks down the hill. Soon they led to a circular stone building at the edge of the marketplace. She had passed the spot earlier, but she hadn't noticed the building. The tall trees surrounding it hid it from view.

As she drew closer, she heard men's voices and the sound of an animal shuffling its feet.

Megan quickly put out the torch so the men wouldn't notice her.

The angry voices grew louder.

"We must start toward Sparta at once," someone was saying. "If we are discovered in Athens with this statue, Antiphon, we will be punished severely."

I was right, Megan thought excitedly. Antiphon and his friend were the thieves!

"I know it is unsafe to linger, Menon," Antiphon replied. "But the dedication of Nestor's temple is being held tomorrow." He chuckled harshly. "And I cannot resist the temptation to stay and see the proud architect's face when he discovers that his precious statue is missing. Demeter will not be so pleased with him then."

"It is time to go," the other man insisted. He sounded nervous and agitated. "Our hiding spot in this sanctuary will be discovered at daybreak."

There was a loud, irritated sigh.

"All right!" Antiphon snapped. "We will leave Athens. But first I must secure the cart."

Megan's pulse quickened. The thieves were leaving! I've got to do something, she told herself frantically.

But what? There were two of them and only one of her. Besides that, Antiphon was about twice her size. A vision of Zeus holding his thunderbolt flashed in her mind. If only she were as powerful as he is, she thought desperately.

Suddenly, an idea popped into her head. She ducked behind one of the wide pillars supporting the marble roof. From her hiding spot, she could see Antiphon and his friend adjusting a donkey's lead rope. Sure enough, the cart held a thick woolen blanket covering a large object. It had to be the missing statue.

Making her voice as deep and tough as she could, Megan called, "Halt!"

Startled, Antiphon stopped and turned around. His eyes anxiously scanned the darkness.

"Who is there?" his friend demanded.

Megan's heart thumped. "I am the messenger of Demeter," she shouted. "The goddess has sent me to tell you that you have greatly displeased her tonight."

"We have displeased the goddess of the harvest?" Antiphon repeated. To Megan's amazement, the tall, strong athlete from Sparta was trembling all over.

A burst of courage shot through her. "Yes," Megan replied. Her voice echoed powerfully through the open-air sanctuary. "If you do not replace that statue and leave Athens at once, you and the other citizens of Sparta will be punished with a long drought."

The other man's eyes were wide with panic. "We only

meant to please the goddess by taking the statue to Sparta," he said pleadingly.

"Please, messenger," Antiphon added. "Demeter must not punish us or Sparta. Last year our city-state suffered a bad winter. Food was very scarce."

"You are acting against Demeter's wishes," Megan's voice thundered. "That statue must be returned to the temple that Nestor and Lysius have built or..." She let her voice trail off ominously. "Beware of Demeter's wrath!"

Without a word, Antiphon grabbed the donkey's lead rope. He took one quick look around, as if he were hoping to catch a glimpse of the invisible messenger from Mount Olympus. Then he and his companion quickly led the donkey away.

Megan stayed hidden in the shadows as the two men passed her hiding spot. But she was so pleased with her performance, she had to cover her mouth to keep from bursting into laughter.

I did it! she thought triumphantly. All on her own, she had managed to persuade the men to return the stolen statue!

Still, she realized, she'd better follow them, just in case they changed their minds.

Chapter Seven

"Good-bye, Ancient Greece"

 egan stayed a short distance behind the men as they climbed the hill. Luckily, there was no sign of Nestor. She didn't know what would happen if he bumped into them as they were returning the statue.

When the men reached the temple, they uncovered the object in the cart. Together they hoisted the statue out and carried it over to the pedestal.

"There." Antiphon grunted as they carefully set it down on the marble base. "This should please the goddess."

The other man nodded. "Let's leave for Sparta tonight," he said in a worried tone. "Just in case someone noticed that the statue was missing for a while."

"Don't be a fool," Antiphon snapped. "It is the middle of the night. Everyone else in Athens is sound asleep!"

Not everyone, Megan thought silently. What would these men say if they knew that someone here was wide awake and watching them right now!

A moment later, they hurried away. They won't be back, Megan said to herself with relief. She waited another few minutes, then went over to the tall pedestal.

It was Megan's first look at the statue. It was of a tall, beautiful woman with long, flowing hair. In her arms were fruit and stalks of wheat. Her eyes looked wise, and her smile was wide and kind. It was obvious to Megan that the sculptor saw Demeter as a friendly and kindhearted ruler.

Megan was so caught up in admiring the statue that she didn't hear someone approaching from behind.

"Megala!" a voice said sharply. "I told you to go home!"

Megan whirled around. Nestor was standing there, his hands on his hips and anger flashing in his eyes.

"Nestor!" Megan burst out. "Wait until you hear this!" She told him about her quick thinking and how she'd frightened Antiphon and his friend.

Nestor's eyes grew wide. "They thought you were a messenger from Demeter?"

Megan nodded proudly.

Nestor was stunned. "I have heard of gods impersonating humans, but never of a human impersonating a messenger from a goddess!" he declared. Then he shook his head and grinned. "I have no idea what my parents would say about your actions tonight, Megala. But I think you are very brave."

Megan's smile grew wider.

"And very smart," Nestor added. "After you left, I searched all around the temple grounds, but I never noticed the tracks."

"See?" Megan couldn't resist saying. "I told you that you might need my help."

"It is true, Megala, but a woman's duties are at home," Nestor said gently. His eyes twinkled as he laughed and shook his head. "Soon you'll be telling me that girls should compete in the games at the Olympic festival, too."

As Nestor took her arm and led her home, Megan stayed quiet, even though she wanted to tell Nestor that someday girls *would* be competing in the Olympics.

The next morning Megan woke to the sounds of people bustling about the house and remembered that it was the start of the Festival of the Eleusinian Mysteries. She dressed and grabbed the feather fan on her way out.

The sun shone high in the clear blue sky, and Megan's gold necklace sparkled below the golden wreath she wore in her hair. Nestor and his father carried ears of corn and tall sickles, symbols of the approaching harvest.

Hundreds of people had already gathered at the *agora*. An official in a long robe was giving a sermon from the beautiful painted porch. He spoke about the people's sacrifices for the Earth Mother Demeter and their hopes that the year's harvest would reap plenty of food for the winter ahead. Megan closed her eyes, offering her own hopes for a bountiful crop.

It was late afternoon before the lead torch bearer, dressed in flowing robes, lifted his flame high overhead and the procession to the temple began. Megan's stomach quivered with nervous excitement as she, Aunt Cassia, and the others lit their own torches. This was the moment that Nestor and Uncle Lysius had been waiting for.

Megan had expected the march to be solemn and silent. Instead, wild shouts rang out on the hillside. To her surprise, many of the men danced and sang even more joyfully when a sudden rain shower drenched the crowd. Megan watched in wonder. She'd never seen

anything quite like this amazing celebration.

At the temple, Uncle Lysius and Nestor proudly stepped to the altar, their eyes glowing. The two architects were the first to lay their gifts at the feet of the gleaming bronze statue of Demeter.

Priests chanted prayers to the goddess as the people of Athens laid down their offerings and moved on toward Eleusis, the sacred site, many miles away.

"I'll catch up with you in a minute," Megan said to Aunt Cassia as she shielded her eyes against the setting sun.

Megan walked back up to the statue of Earth Mother. She wanted one last look at Demeter's smile. Resting her hand on the statue's feet, she examined every detail of the huge figure, then looked out toward the procession of worshipers. Their torches glowed like brilliant fireflies dancing on the hillside.

At the base of the pedestal someone had placed a small, round carving. One side was decorated with a scene of the gods of Olympus. The other side had been polished to a bright shine. Megan gazed down at her reflection and the rolling hills of Athens faded away. The next thing she knew she was back in Ellie's attic, the soft patter of rain beating on the roof overhead.

Chapter
Eight

BACK HOME

 egan folded the white and gold *chiton* and matching cape. Carefully, she placed the outfit back in the trunk. Then she turned out the overhead light and headed downstairs to find her friend.

Ellie was in the kitchen snipping sprigs of fresh parsley into a small bowl. "Hi, Megan," she said cheerfully. "How was your time in the attic?"

"Wonderful, Ellie!" Megan took a seat at the kitchen table. "I found a white and gold tunic in the trunk, and I traveled to ancient Greece!"

Megan told Ellie all about her adventure. When she got to the part about how she'd stopped Antiphon from stealing the statue, Ellie's mouth dropped open. "That was very quick and clever of you, Megan," she declared. "You're a true Greek hero."

Megan smiled. "Everything was so different back then," she explained. "The girls and women didn't go out of the house very much, unless they were servants. Girls like Penelope got married when they were only fourteen or fifteen." She shook her head. "That's not much older than I am!"

"Times have certainly changed, haven't they?" Ellie said.

"I'll say," Megan declared. Now that she was back home, she realized she was grateful for many things about modern life—including her family's cars, their computers, the telephone. "I'm even lucky to go to school every day," Megan declared, making Ellie laugh.

As Ellie poured the hot vegetable soup she had been making into plastic containers, Megan stared out the window. The sky was still gray, and the rain was still coming down. "I guess not everything has changed since ancient times," she said thoughtfully.

Ellie looked up. "What do you mean?"

"I mean, if Mother Nature wants rain, it's going to rain."
Ellie nodded sympathetically.

"I was so angry about it this morning, but now..."
Megan shrugged, then smiled a small smile.

A short while later Megan ran home through the
downpour, carrying a container of soup that Ellie had
sent along for her family. As Megan dashed up her front
steps, she saw her four best friends standing on the front
porch. They were about to ring her bell.

"Here she comes!" Rose yelled.

"Hi, Megan!" Heather called. In her arms was a tall
stack of board games.

"We're sorry the hayride was cancelled," Keisha said.
"Your Aunt Frances said you were really disappointed this
morning."

"So we came over to cheer you up," Rose finished.

Megan smiled. "I'm glad you came, guys. But guess what?"

"What?" Alison asked.

"I don't need to be cheered up anymore."

"You don't?" Keisha said, surprised.

Heather peered at Megan. "You went to Ellie's attic,
didn't you?" she asked, grinning slyly.

"I sure did," Megan exclaimed. "And I can't wait to tell
you about my adventure!" Eagerly, she pushed open the
front door. Everyone trooped inside, where it was warm

and dry, and they had a whole afternoon to spend together.

Diary

Dear Diary,

   I hate to admit it, but I was completely wrong! The other fifth-graders were disappointed about the hayride, but they loved Mr. Appleby's suggestion about visiting the pumpkin patch. We just got back from his farm and everyone (including me) had a great time. We picked pumpkins, ate spider cookies and ghost cupcakes, and told spooky stories in the barn. But the best part was riding around the farm on the antique fire truck and clanging that silly bell. Keisha and Joey Diaz said that they haven't had that much fun since kindergarten!

   Thanksgiving is just a few weeks away, and this year I'm really looking forward to it. It's very different from the Greeks' festival to honor the goddess of the harvest, but in a way we're celebrating the earth and the food on our tables, too. This year I'm thankful for many things, especially my friends, my family, and Ellie's delicious homemade soup!

Love,

Megan